Flood Find

Jan Barrow

Illustrations by Robin Lawrie

First Impression—1996
Second Impression—1999

ISBN 1 85902 326 6

© Jan Barrow

This book is published with the support of the Arts Council of Wales

Printed in Wales at
Gomer Press, Llandysul, Dyfed.

For
Raiza and Thomas

Acknowledgements

Thanks are due to the Custodian and staff,
Roman Legionary Museum, Caerleon, Gwent

Chapter One

Gareth was digging. He had been digging since breakfast and now the rumbles in his stomach told him it was time for elevenses. He paused, wiped a dollop of mud from his glasses and looked down into the hole he was digging and at the pile of things he had unearthed. It was an odd collection; old sardine tins, a kettle with no bottom, bed springs, bits of bicycle, a saucepan, a mousetrap and even a bit of an old wireless set. He sighed. Nothing yet to shout about.

Gareth knew the digging was necessary for he was planning to become an archaeologist when he grew up and most ancient things seem to end up under tons of earth. Ever since his class visited the Museum in Cardiff last summer he had wanted to know more and more about people and animals who had lived hundreds and even thousands of years ago. He was practising ready for the time when he could become a real archaeologist; and who knows, he might find something round the farm—he might even find it today!

It was Mam's idea that he should dig on the other side of the garden wall by the old farm. She said it had been used as a rubbish dump for years and years in the days before plastic sacks and binmen, and besides he wouldn't dig up her rhubarb and bulbs if he kept out of the garden.

Gareth wasn't too excited by his morning's finds but thought he'd carry on a bit longer till Mam was back in the kitchen. She might have more flapjack stored away that she could unearth for elevenses; his stomach gave another hopeful rumble at the thought. He could see her red woolly hat bobbing about in the barn where she was feeding the orphan baby lambs with bottles. He kept shovelling steadily, his thoughts full of ancient tombs and skeletons and swords and shields. He was so wrapped up that he scarcely heard the mountain sounds: the bleating of the sheep, Dad's tractor chugging up the hillside, Mam's hens telling the world that they'd laid an egg, a dog barking, and far away a plane droning its lonely way north.

Suddenly his spade clinked on something metal. He dropped his spade and scraped at the earth with his fingers until he touched something shiny and round. It was quite different from the usual things he found. Could it be an unexploded bomb? Gareth paused and thought for a bit. No, it couldn't be a bomb, not in the rubbish dump. The round shape came loose at last. Gareth laughed. It was a British soldier's old tin hat from World War II. He decided to clean it up and try it on, so hoisting his skinny legs out of the hole he pushed his glasses more firmly onto his nose (they always slipped down when he was digging) and hurried off to the back kitchen.

The back kitchen was a real glory hole where the boots and old coats were kept, and the farm cats lurked when they didn't want to be turned out at night. It had blue stone slabs instead of tables and was always cold. Mam said years ago people made butter in there and salted a pig for the winter, but now she used it for washing out the lambs' bottles. It was just the place for washing mud off his finds too.

The tin hat took quite a bit of scrubbing out, but after a last rinse under the tap Gareth wiped it on an old sock he found in a gumboot, and put it on his head. He looked at himself in the mirror. The hat was so big that it came down over his ears and with his spectacles he looked like a monster insect. He stuck his tongue out and tried to decide what species he belonged to.

A bucket clattered outside; Mam was coming in.

I'll make Mam laugh, thought Gareth. He grabbed a walking stick and stood behind the door holding the stick like a rifle.

'Halt, who goes there?' he shouted in his gruffest voice.

'*Duw mawr,*' cried Mam nearly jumping out of her skin and letting go a new lamb which slid down her anorak and bleated loudly at Gareth's feet.

'Whatever are you doing, boy? I nearly had a turn. And what is that terrible smell?' Mam sniffed suspiciously at Gareth. 'It's Tada's old army hat from the War! 'We used it upside down for a dog's bowl for years. Oh take it out, Gareth, I want to wash the lambs' feeding bottles.'

Gareth realised Mam wasn't in a laughing mood. She began peeling off her anorak and some of her woollies now that she was indoors again. Her dark curly hair was escaping from her woolly hat and her cheeks were rosy from the cold wind on the mountainside.

'Be a good lad and go and put the kettle on, I'm dying for a cup of tea. Watching those lambs guzzling milk has made me thirsty too! And go and find some clean trousers before you even think of sitting down!'

Gareth went and switched on the kettle and poured himself a glass of milk. Mam just wasn't interested in old things. How he wished Tadcu still lived with them. Tada knew about everything old on the farm, and even broken bits of harness and chain could be explained by Tada. But Tada's legs had become too wobbly with rheumatism to go up and

11

down stairs in the old farm and he'd had to go and live with Auntie Rhiannon in her bungalow in Crickhowell. Tada had been born on the farm and he loved to talk of old times before the days of tractors and TV. He didn't make fun of the archaeology either; he said Gareth took after great Uncle Tudur who taught history in the Grammar School fifty years ago. Gareth did miss Tada. He would know all about the tin hat and he had wonderful stories about the War when he was a soldier.

Gareth crept quietly upstairs to his bedroom in the farm attic. At least no one bothered him up there and he was quite used to doing things on his own, living so far up in the hills. Sometimes in the summer his best school friend Gethin came on Saturdays and they had a great time birdwatching and making hides with rocks and bracken so that the birds couldn't see them. They even saw a red kite once, well Gethin said it was one, but as they had forgotten to take their bird book they couldn't be really sure. Sometimes they took a feast with them. The best ones always had a tin of Heinz beans, cold sausages and tomato sauce with big apple turnovers for afters.

But bird watching was only his second best hobby now since archaeology had taken over and the problem was that Gethin wasn't interested in digging. Plus his mother created if he got muddy—even more than Gareth's.

Gareth often talked things over with Caradoc, although he made a better listener than talker. Caradoc liked the attic although Gareth suspected that it had something to do with the scuttlings and rustlings in the roof above. This morning Caradoc was curled up on his pillow with his stripy tail neatly covering his nose. He opened his big green eyes for a second and then settled himself more deeply into the pillow. He wasn't in a listening mood any more than Mam.

Gareth often took little snacks for Caradoc up into his attic. Sometimes he rescued a mouse from one of the farm cats for him but Caradoc's favourite snack was sardines. The trouble was they made rather a smell, and then Mam would start cleaning and re-arranging things. Only last week she had thrown out two perfectly good Hob Nob biscuits she said were stale. They weren't stale at all, only a bit fluffy.

So Gareth looked over his shelf full of the things he had dug up round the farm. Perhaps one day I'll find some that are hundreds and hundreds of years old, he thought. He ran his fingers over the nails and hooks, chains and bits of harness and the little clay pipes and old green glass bottles he had found, and dreamt about the men who must have smoked the pipes and drunk beer out of the bottles a hundred years ago.

A heavy clumping on the attic stairs brought him back to the present; his brother David was shouting to him.

'Gareth! Dinner time—we've called you twice. Come *on* will you and leave your treasure!'

David clattered away down the stairs. David isn't a bit interested in history either—all he can think about is computers, thought Gareth. He hurried down. A delicious smell of roast lamb and mint sauce was coming from the kitchen. Dad was at the big kitchen table, the knife in his strong brown hands, expertly carving the joint while Mam bustled over with a dish of roast potatoes done to a turn in the Aga cooker. Dad insisted on a roast for Sunday dinner although Mam loved trying out new recipes on the family. Gareth's favourite was pasta with lots of tomato sauce and cheese and Mam could do great stir fries too, especially if she had been to the town twelve miles away and got all the right bits from Tescos.

There was a squeal of brakes in the farmyard. Mam stopped by the window on her way back to the Aga for the gravy.

'My goodness, who is that with Bethan?' she exclaimed. The car screeched away and Bethan burst into the kitchen.

'I'm not late for dinner am I? Mr Thomas wasn't there today and I had to beg another lift home.'

'Well, the driver was very good looking, *cariad*. Is it a new boyfriend?' Mam just loved to know about the latest of Bethan's friends.

Bethan tossed her black curls. Gareth supposed she was very pretty, with her big brown eyes, pale skin and slim figure, well Mam said she was. She always had boy friends phoning or calling for her. Gareth couldn't think what they saw in her, she was always so grumpy with him. Either he was in the way, dirty, earwigging on her phone conversations, or was in the bathroom when she wanted it. The bathroom grump just wasn't true. Gareth did his best to save water by washing only once a day, and using the bathroom for no more than five minutes at a time.

Gareth was always a bit dirty. Mam said he was the only boy she'd ever known who could get dirty in bed asleep. Well, sometimes Caradoc came into bed for company and his paws might be a bit muddy. Then there were the midnight snacks he made for himself so that he wouldn't starve in the night, and Marmite did make brown streaks on the sheets. One night his racing snails Sid and Sam got out of their box and trundled across his pillow leaving a gooey trail. When Mam found them that had caused a big bother. But then all mothers created about dirt. They seemed not to feel real mothers unless they did.

The curl-tossing ceased and Bethan laughed at Mam's nosiness. 'No, it was just a visitor at the hotel going north to Shrewsbury, so it was only a bit out of his way to drop me off.'

Bethan had a weekend job in the big hotel in the valley and she helped serve breakfasts and make beds before she came home.

'Do you lot want to eat today or shall we put all this back in the oven until next week?' Poor Dad was getting impatient with all the chatter. He'd been out in the hills since 6 o'clock in the morning and was very hungry.

David had been sitting saying nothing all this time. He never said much to anyone, as though his brain was in a high tower and only occasionally sent messages to ground level. He had a vastly superior look on his face and obviously felt himself above the female chat about boyfriends. All he could think of was A levels and computers and university. Gareth sometimes wondered if he would rather have a floppy disc for dinner than meat and vegetables. And when he did speak it all seemed to be about kilobites, ASCII files and parameters. Now he rattled the pile of plates and started passing them one by one to Dad who had been getting on with the carving and was ready to put slices on the plates.

Dinner was delicious and they all tucked in happily. As the empty stomachs filled up conversation started again. 'You're very quiet, Gareth,' said Dad. 'What were you doing down by the garden wall? I saw you from up the mountain.'

'Oh well, nothing much,' mumbled Gareth, 'just digging a bit.' He waited for the usual jeers from David and Bethan, but was saved by Mam tripping over one of the cats and nearly dropping the custard saucepan.

'Are there any new lambs this morning?' asked Mam when she had shouted at the cat and calmed down a bit.

'Yes and more to come soon,' said Dad. 'I hope the weather won't turn wet or we may lose the weak ones.'

He put down his knife and fork and sighed. Dad never said a great deal; he was a quiet man who spent long lonely days on the mountain with his hundreds of sheep and he loved the mountains and his farm. He saw very few people except on market and sale days. Gareth couldn't imagine his Dad exchanging his cord trousers, battered old hat and Land Rover for a suit and brief case and a posh shiny car.

'Gareth, bring the pudding dishes for me, *bach*,' said Mam.

As he crossed over to the dresser he looked through the window.

'Gosh, look at the sky!' he cried.

They all got up and peered out; the sky was the most peculiar leaden colour and the rocks on the mountain stood out stark and desolate like a moonscape.

'I don't like the look of that,' said Dad. 'Let's put the weather forecast on and see what we are in for.' David switched the telly on and the green map of Wales appeared heavily dotted with rain spots and big black clouds. The weather forecast was just dreadful; Monday and Tuesday with gales and very heavy rain over the mountains of mid Wales and flooding expected in the valleys.

Dad went out with David to make sure the sheep were all right and to fasten down anything that looked as though it might blow away. Mam got the candles and lamps ready in case the overhead electricity wires came down. Gareth was a bit scared. It seemed as though everyone was expecting something quite terrible in the way of weather.

Tucked up safely beneath his blankets that night, Gareth began to wonder what the storm would do. Perhaps the gales would blow down old buildings and reveal hidden passages and even walled-up skeletons. Perhaps the floods would wash away tons of soil in the valley and show the remains of ancient buildings; perhaps archaeologists would come to his valley from all over Wales; from all over Britain; from all over Europe; from all over the world . . .

Chapter Two

The storm came in the early hours of the morning. They were woken up by the noise of thunder, the blue flashing of lightning and rain bucketing down. The rain came down harder and harder, rattling like machine-gun fire on the barn roof. Great gusts of wind blew round the old buildings and there were crashes as loose slates were torn from the barn and buckets and tins clattered round the farm yard. But worst of all was the wind howling and moaning down the big chimney like a lost spirit.

No one could sleep with such a din outside and Mam got up to make tea and cocoa to comfort them all, and to let in Ben who hated thunder.

The old dog went straight under the sofa and buried his head in Mam's knitting bag he found there. Then Dad went downstairs worrying about the sheep in the bottom fields.

'If this goes on the river will be in flood and sheep will be drowned,' he said to Mam.

By about 4 o'clock the storm quietened and they all managed to drop off to sleep again for a few hours. But when morning came no one wanted to get up, they were so tired. Gareth lay looking up through the skylight in his attic bedroom; the grey square of glass was streaming with water and he wondered for one dreadful moment if the floods had reached the roof of the farm. He jumped out of bed and went down to the next landing to look out of that window. It was all right, the farm wasn't under water, but the daffodils in the garden were squashed flat by the rain and the brook beside the farm was leaping wildly down the hillside in a foaming waterfall. In the valley below, the river looked twice its normal size.

Breakfast was late; everyone was grumpy after an almost sleepless night. 'Need we bother to go for the school bus?' asked Bethan yawning her head off. But Mam didn't allow staying at home unless things were desperate.

'The school bus usually gets through,' she said. 'Have a good breakfast now to keep the damp out.' But the three of them hadn't time for more than toast, and they half-heartedly struggled into their wet weather clothes ready to walk the three quarters of a mile down to their buses on the main road.

'There won't be any football today, that's for sure,' said David, pointing down to the valley as they walked down the hillside. 'Just look at those fields. And the tree trunks floating like canoes! But our sheep are all right at the moment as long as the river bank doesn't burst.'

'What about those poor sheep on that island all on

21

their own?' said Bethan 'Look there's a boat and some men; it must be too deep for the sheep to walk!'

Gareth was too busy looking where he was putting his feet to gaze at distant sheep. His spectacles were awash with the rain and he could hardly see where he was going. Why hadn't anyone invented spectacle wipers like car windscreen wipers? Gareth wondered if he could invent some and become famous. He would need little wipers, some wire and a torch battery for power, and a sort of head frame to hold it all together.

He was so busy thinking about his future invention that he forgot to look where he was going and blundered into a deep puddle which splashed Bethan from head to toe.

'You idiot,' she yelled. She really was disagreeable this morning.

The school buses were late. While they waited Gareth tested the puddles. Some came almost to the top of his gum boots. He watched the rainwater tumbling down the mountainside. It formed little waterfalls over the rocks and there were dozens of them foaming and sparkling down the steep slopes making a rushing, plashing sound. Gareth thought he could hear every water sound except sea waves. There was the rain pattering, the splashing of the waterfalls, the brook racing and gurgling along and as a background to it all, the deep angry roar of the main river.

There was a dead mole by the roadside. Gareth supposed it had been drowned in its burrow. It seemed a very small creature to make such huge mole hills. He had a good look at it now: he hardly ever saw a live one, just the mole hill wobbling. He and Caradoc had waited a whole hour once, but the mole never popped up.

Half an hour later they were still at the bus stop. They stood huddled together with their backs to the rain which was still coming down in great sheets of water. No cars were coming down the road at all, only a couple of tractors with water up to their axles and the road was beginning to look like a canal.

'This is stupid' said David. 'We'd have done better to stay at home and help Dad with the sheep. I think we'd better go back to the farm.'

Bethan was only too glad to agree with him. 'I wish Mam hadn't been so keen to send us off this morning. We must be the only ones in the valley stuck like three idiots at a bus stop.'

Back they went up the lane, too tired and wet to care whether they splashed each other.

They had got halfway home when Dad came trundling into sight on the tractor with Ben and

Cymro perched up beside him out of the water. 'Good, you had the sense to come back,' said Dad. 'We've just had a phone call from Bob Parry next door to say the school bus can't get through.'

'We've just about gathered that, Dad! There aren't any cars either, the water must be too deep. I'll give you a hand with the sheep, shall I?' said David and opened the field gate to let Dad through with the tractor.

Bethan and Gareth carried on back to the farm. The kitchen was warm and steamy with wet clothes and wet baby lambs. Mam was drinking a mug of hot tea.

'Dear me, what a morning. Did you see your Father down there? Is David helping him?' Wearily Bethan and Gareth nodded. 'Now come and have a proper breakfast then. We're lucky we didn't lose the electricity. Then you can come and help me with the baby lambs and their bottles, both of you.'

'Oh Mam, do we have to?' grumbled Bethan, 'I've got a dreadful headache. And we needn't have gone out this morning after all!'

Gareth stuck his tongue out after her as she tottered upstairs pretending to feel awful. Her bedroom door banged shut. He knew the minute Mam's back was turned she's be on the phone to her best friend Rhian Lewis, fantasising about being air hostesses. The headache was just an excuse to get out of helping with the lambs. Bethan hated farm work.

Why was it, Gareth asked himself, that horrible older sisters were obviously so wonderful for someone else's older brothers? Then they got married and had boy and girl babies and it all started over again. He'd never heard of anyone with a nice older sister, and he reckoned Bethan could win prizes in a Nasty Sister Competition—a National one at that.

'Well, one of you must come, I'm up to my ears with lambs,' said Mam crossly and hurried off into the yard.

Gareth had just got his boots back on when the phone rang. He picked up the receiver.

'Morgan, Graig Allt Farm,' he said in his best telephone voice.

'Can I speak to Bethan?' Gareth recognised the voice of Bethan's latest admirer, a loud show-off sort of bloke with a motor bike. Dad didn't approve of the boy nor the motor bike.

'Oh, I'm afraid she's not well,' said Gareth sadly, 'in fact she's had to go to bed with a terrible headache. I don't think she could possibly get up.'

'Oh,' said the voice, and rang off without even saying goodbye.

Gareth chuckled to himself, and crept out quickly as he heard Bethan shouting downstairs, 'Who was that, was it for me?'

By the time they'd finished feeding the lambs Dad and David were back from the bottom fields and they'd helped their neighbour Bob Parry move his sheep to higher land too.

'Thank goodness we've got the near flock into the barn and none are missing,' said Dad, 'but I'm worried about the ones further up the mountain too. It's very exposed for any small lambs in weather like this. As soon as we've had a hot drink we'll take the dogs and go and check on the rest of the flock.'

They split up into two parties; Dad and David with old Ben, and Mam with the young dog Cymro. 'You can go with your Mam,' said Dad to Bethan, 'this is more important than your blessed homework, headache or whatever the excuse is; it's the family's livelihood!' This was an outburst for Dad, who seldom let his worries show. Then he added, more reasonably as if he were sorry for being so sharp with Bethan, 'With this year's finances as they are, we can't afford losses, see, Beth.' For once, Bethan did as she was told and didn't cheek Dad back.

'What about me?' said Gareth feeling left out.

'You stay here and hold the fort,' said Dad, 'and

keep an eye on the lambs. And you could listen for the phone as well.'

'Keep the local radio on too, *cariad*, it will tell us what is happening with the floods,' said Mam as she tied her anorak hood firmly under her chin ready to set off into the rain.

They all hurried off with the dogs, without even waiting for him to reply. Gareth sighed. Well, he was used to being the odd one. Suddenly a gnawing pain which he immediately identified as hunger attacked his insides. It needed instant attention.

There was a lonely looking jam tart in the larder, a big crusty loaf and lots of cheese. It tasted wonderful. In spite of being skinny Gareth did eat a lot. In fact he was almost always hungry and the archaeological digging seemed to make him even hungrier. Mam said he burnt up his calories fast. None of his friends seemed to need as much food as he did. He planned to join a Hungry Persons Society as soon as he could find one. They might have advisers and he could write a letter asking how to survive longer without so much food. He'd already written to BBC *Blue Peter* for their ideas on the problem and was waiting for their reply. He scooped the last crumbs from his plate and thought about what he should do next.

The two baby lambs in a box near the Aga were

asleep. Three of the farm cats had crept in from the rain and were squeezed up against the Aga; they were snoozing too.

They don't need me, thought Gareth. I'll go and start a List of my Finds. He went up the attic stairs and after giving Caradoc a few cuddles he got out his new notebook, a present from Tada specially for the List. He had a new blue biro too.

The next hour was spent writing his List. He had separate pages for different groups of Finds.

Bottles	:	3 all in the same green glass
Bottles	:	1 blue one with fluted sides and the word POISON on it
Keys	:	4 rusty small ones
Marbles	:	1 green glass, 2 clay, 1 alley
Clay pipe	:	1 whole one with J.Jones Newport stamped on the bowl
Clay pipe	:	6 plain ones with no names
Coins	:	1 Victorian penny 1893 and one penny 1850
Nails	:	6 iron ones, all rather bent
Horseshoes:		5 all different sizes, very worn

Gareth paused for a bit. He couldn't think how to list the bits of chain and pieces of broken pottery and china.

He felt he deserved a little rest after all the neat writing, so he opened his new book on archaeology. It was a wonderful book, with illustrations, lots of them, diagrams and explanations and even maps. It was the most expensive book he had ever owned. He almost hadn't been able to afford it but Tada had given him a £20 note at Christmas as well as a skateboard. Gareth's savings always seemed to be eaten away by something or other. The cost of living was very expensive for boys these days, even a decent sized bun cost 40p and you couldn't get a Mars bar for 30p any more, not a full-size one anyway. And then there was the recent bother with Caradoc and the fish for supper. Caradoc had got into the larder, had a feast on the fish and then been sick. Gareth was having to pay a fine of 10p a week towards the next fish supper, as Mam had proved without any shadow of doubt that it was Gareth who had left the larder door open.

As he opened his book he soon forgot the farm and the floods. How fantastic, he thought to himself, to find chests full of Inca gold in South America and pharaohs' tombs and mummies (he wondered why they weren't daddies too) in Egypt. Or a house buried under lava near an old volcano in Italy. A Viking helmet in Britain or perhaps some crosses and things stolen from a monastery and buried would be exciting. Or even a few pottery bowls if they were old. He looked at his shelf of bottles and nails and clay pipes; it did look a bit ordinary. 'But I only started six months ago,' he said to himself. 'Some archaeologists have to search for years and years.'

He looked up at his bedroom skylight and saw that the sky seemed lighter, so it had actually stopped raining at last. He went downstairs and all was peaceful in the kitchen. The old grandfather clock ticked steadily, the Aga was hot, and the animals were still dozing with just the occasional twitch of their ears. Gareth looked at the clock—the others had been gone two hours. He was sick of being cooped up in the farmhouse.

Then he had an idea: perhaps he should go and see if he could see any sheep too. Why not? And Dad would be more than pleased if all his flock was safe.

Gareth looked at the sleeping animals and made up his mind. Yes, he'd go and look around for sheep too. Quickly he put on his boots still damp from the morning, and his waterproof jacket and yellow sou'wester. He gave a last glance at the quiet kitchen, shut the door carefully behind him, and set off up the mountain.

The mountain above looked bleak and its top was

covered in gloomy cloud and rain. Gareth felt no one would have wanted to live up there amongst the rocks so there couldn't possibly be anything archaeological there. Well, probably not, anyway.

Chapter Three

Gareth looked down into the valley. The river had spread into the fields along its banks; the mountain stream still splashed wildly downwards and every time Gareth moved, his boots sank into the ground and squelched. He couldn't see any sheep left on the mountain, nor could he see his family with the sheepdogs. He was a mountain boy and stood and listened, for on the mountain sounds carry a long way. But all he could hear was the splashing stream and water dripping from the rocks and gorse bushes. He walked on further, listening and looking up the mountain. His farm showed small and white in the rain mists below.

While he kept his eyes open for sheep his thoughts were about archaeology. Would the the rain and floods in the valley really wash earth away to show parts of old buried buildings, he wondered to himself.

Suddenly out of the corner of his eye he saw a movement; it was small and pale, a tiny lamb. Gareth hurried towards the spot at least a hundred metres away above him. And rounding a corner of rock, he stopped in amazement. An overhanging ledge and the stone and earth above it had fallen. It was a small landslide.

I expect all the rain loosened something and it just collapsed, thought Gareth. Then he heard a familiar sound, 'Maa,' it went. It was the tiny lamb, shivering and frightened. Gareth, now every bit the sheep farmer's son, picked it up and put it inside his jacket to warm it.

'Where's your Mam, then?' he said to the little woolly face. The lamb snuggled down in the warmth and bleated again.

Gareth realised that the poor ewe was probably under the earth and rock. She might even be dead. What should he do? While he stood trying to make up his mind, he heard another sound, a very faint 'Baa' from inside the rocks. The lamb bleated frantically and struggled to get out.

'Well, she isn't dead. I'd better just see if I can see her,' he said to himself.

The rain was starting to fall again from the grey sky and Gareth shivered. Then, making up his mind, he started climbing up and round the side of the landslide. It wouldn't do for him to be buried as well as the sheep. The Baas got louder and Gareth put the lamb down on the hillside. It bleated and ran towards a rock face which looked solid, then just disappeared.

When Gareth reached the rock, he could see a narrow slit. The tiny lamb had scrambled in and out,

but the fat, woolly ewe could only get her head through the gap. At least she wasn't hurt, only upset. Perhaps he could let her out. Gareth started scraping away at the earth with his hands. It was harder than he thought so he found a flattish piece of rock and used it like a trowel. There was more rock than he had bargained for too, but at last he gave a good shove at the last big chunk which was in the way . . . and fell headlong into a small cave on top of the ewe.

Gareth struggled to his feet and groped around for his glasses. They were lying across the lamb's ears like goggles making it look like Snoopy, but at least they weren't broken. He looked at the cave-opening anxiously. There was room for him to get out, thank goodness, but the poor ewe was still too fat.

The daylight was going fast now and it was almost dark in the cave but he could stand upright in it and it seemed to go back a bit further. Gareth peered into the darkness; it did look interesting. He felt about in the inner pocket of his waterproof jacket for his electric torch. Mam made everyone on the farm carry a torch in their pocket during the winter because the lane up to the farm was very dark. He found the torch, which thankfully had lots of power left in its battery, and started inspecting the cave.

It was only just high enough for Gareth to stand upright. The rough walls had marks on them, as though a pick or a hammer had taken out chunks, leaving dark, metallic dents. He ran his hand over the nearest wall and found that it was covered with dark, reddish dust. Quickly, he shone his torch-light all the way round the cave, straining his eyes to see its limits. There were little passages worked into the walls, but when he explored them with the torch-beam they didn't seem to go anywhere. There were holes, too, in the rock walls. He peered in and saw that inside they were black, as though candles or lamps had burned in them once.

Gareth had a sudden feeling that this wasn't just an old sheep shelter; this was something much older. He crept round the cave inspecting every nook and cranny. He forgot he was hungry, he forgot the sheep, the rain, and the floods. Somehow he just KNEW he was discovering something which had been hidden for hundreds of years. But he still couldn't work out what the passages were for— perhaps this was an old quarry? But Dad and Tada had never mentioned it and the farm and the mountainside had been in the family for nearly four hundred years.

He looked at the nooks for lamps. There was no candle grease, but the black stuff was like soot. Odd, he thought to himself. Then he found another nook, a roughly cut one behind an overhanging rock. It had something in it. A little lamp made of some sort of pottery. It looked like the lamps they used in that Aladdin pantomime he had seen on TV—but that was in Arabia or some place thousands of miles away: this was Wales. Full of curiosity he felt around the hole again and in one corner a small piece of rock came away in his hand. Behind it was yet another hole and inside it a pot about the size of a small teapot.

Gareth held his breath and lifted it out. He set it gently on the ground and he looked at it. It had a slit on top and a sort of stopper underneath. He shook it slightly and it rattled. Whatever could be inside? Cautiously he removed the stopper, thinking about genies escaping—after all, there was a lamp by the pot! But out tumbled a handful of dull purple black coins the size of 1p pieces.

Gareth sat back on his heels, his heart thumping with excitement. So this was what it felt like to be an archaeologist making a discovery. It was the most thrilling feeling in the world!

But who had left the coins and when? And why? And why hadn't they come back for them?

Suddenly the sheep behind him leapt to their feet and bleated loudly. Far away he could hear dogs barking. Gareth came back to the present with a start. It was Dad with the dogs. He grabbed the little lamb and pushed it through the gap in the rock, and started to shout 'Dad, Dad, I'm here, and look what I've found!'

Chapter Four

'Dad, here's a new lamb, but where's the ewe? Gosh Dad, there's been a landslide, the ewe must be inside!' Wet and tired, David shone his torch over the fallen rock and earth.

His father gave a shout, 'Look at the dogs!' they were whining and scratching at the rock where the ewe's nose had poked out again.

'Dad, here's Gareth's hat' shouted David picking up the old yellow sou'wester Gareth had been wearing.

'Oh God, he could be crushed,' said Dad, his voice grim. The dogs scrabbled madly at the slit in the rock with earth and bits of stone tumbling round them. 'Ben, Cymro, no! Lie down! Let's call into the hole' he said.

But there was no need, a faint voice came out 'Dad, Dad, I'm in here. And Dad I've found something, there's a cave in here, and I've found ...'

'Never mind what you've found, come out before the rest of the hillside falls on you.'

Gareth squeezed out, covered in red dust and mud, blinking in the strong light from the torches. Then Dad and David made the gap a bit wider to let out the fat woolly ewe.

'Wait till your Mam sees you! She thought you'd

gone down to the river and been drowned. The neighbours are out looking for you and she's ready to phone the Police!'

'Dad, I found the ewe and the sheep. And it was so exciting in there. I found . . .'

'I don't care what you found, Gareth. Do you realise how much trouble you've caused just going off on your own like that!'

'But, Dad—' began Gareth.

'Be quiet!' Gareth had never had Dad so angry with him, his Dad who was usually so calm and kind.

'Let's get home all of us, and call off the search.' Dad hurried them, dogs, sheep and all, down the mountain track back to the farm.

'What was it you found, then, the skeleton of an old sheep millions of years old?' David asked scornfully. 'I suppose you know we've been looking for you for two hours up the mountain in the dark!'

Gareth walked downhill behind Dad and David and the dogs with the pale shapes of the sheep gleaming in the beam of Dad's powerful lamp. He was simply hopping with indignation. He hadn't been lost! He could easily have found his way back to the farm with his torch and one could see the lights in the farmhouse window for miles! He'd found the sheep for Dad too. Why couldn't Dad be a bit more grateful instead of shouting at him like that!

And no one wanted to hear about the cave and what he'd found.

Mam and Bethan were waiting at the door. Mam was really cross. Firstly for leaving the farmhouse and not leaving a note, secondly about wandering up the mountain on his own in stormy weather, and thirdly for getting covered in mud again. But Mam had a warm heart as well as a quick temper and the scolding ended in a hug and instructions to go and have a hot bath and get some dry clothes.

Gareth rushed up to his attic room. Caradoc greeted him with a loud 'miaow' and tried to climb up his legs until he found how wet Gareth's jeans were. His spectacles were spotty with rain and dust from the cave and he had to give them a good wipe before he could see Caradoc properly.

'Just look what I've found!' he said and emptied the pot onto the bed. There were dozens of coins; some turned black as they were poured out, but inside there were lots of silver ones and then came six shiny yellow ones. Perhaps,—surely they *were*, gold?

Gareth was shaking from head to foot with excitement, but he was freezing cold too. He pulled off his wet muddy clothes and scuttled along to the bathroom deciding a whole bath was rather necessary for once. He threw in a good dollop of Mam's bath essence. She would be in an even better mood if he smelt nice and clean.

When he came downstairs Mam was laying the supper table. 'Thank goodness we've got Gareth safe and sound, all the sheep plus Gareth's lamb, no one has been drowned and there's no more rain forecast,' Mam said, all cheerful again.

But Dad was sitting in his big chair by the fire with his eyes closed. He looked very tired. Gareth felt a bit guilty. He fidgeted by Dad's chair for a minute, then he bent down and whispered 'Sorry' in Dad's ear.

Dad opened his eyes. 'OK, Gareth, but leave a note before you go off next time.' He smiled.

Gareth knew he and Dad were all right again.

Bethan was making herself really useful with the frying pan. A delicious smell of sausages and bacon was coming from the Aga, and there was another smell too. Ooh! pizza with lots of cheese. Gareth licked his lips. Supper was rounded off with a big rice pudding which had cooked slowly in the Aga since the morning and Gareth had the best bits, the crisp brown scrapings from round the edges. Being the youngest was good in one way, because Bethan didn't want scrapes or seconds because of her figure, and David was far too high and mighty to bag scrapings.

David, coming down to earth for a moment suddenly remembered his brother's excitement on coming out of the rock fall.

'Gareth, what did you find in the landslide?'

Gareth got up from the table without a word and went up to his attic room. He came down again slowly. In his hands he held the strange pot he had found in the rock cave. He put it on the table and waited for his family to say something. He didn't have to wait long.

'Not another of your stupid finds!' Bethan was rude as always.

'A present from the fairies!' scoffed David.

'It looks like my Aunty Gwen's old cooking pot, *bach*!' laughed Mam.

'It's not worth much by the look of it,' said Dad calmly.

Gareth said nothing at all. Instead he took the stopper out of the pot and let the gold coins drop onto the table. The gold glittered in the lamplight.

'*Duw*, they look like gold,' exclaimed Mam.

'Where did you say you found them?' Dad was amazed.

And for the first time for months David and Bethan were speechless.

'They were all in this pot on a rock shelf behind a loose piece of rock,' explained Gareth. 'It looked as though someone had hidden it, and there was a funny little lamp there too. Look there's more, but they're not gold,' and Gareth tipped out all the coins onto the supper table.

'I wonder if they are silver?' said David, recovering from his surprise, 'or bits of tin.'

They all started turning the coins over and looking at them.

'What king or queen's head have they got?' asked Dad.

'They've got a man's head,—I think,' said Bethan peering at a gold coin. 'He's got a funny sort of hairdo like a pony tail. And on the other side there's a man with a helmet on and wings, and he's holding a tool of some sort and yuk, there's a snake, I think.'

David poked at the dingy metal coins 'There's a man's head on these too, but the other side's got a mermaid sort of creature with a fish tail and horns and it's holding a large ball or something.' He yawned. 'I'm too tired to look any more. Tell you what Gareth I'll take them to school for you and ask Mrs. Howells' History. She'll know.'

'No' shouted Gareth. It was his find not David's! 'No, I found them, and I want to do the finding out.

45

You're always making fun of my archaeology and now you want to take over!'

'OK, keep your hair on, I was only trying to help!' At least David backed down quickly.

'Yes indeed, it's Gareth's find. I expect you have plans for it, haven't you?' said Dad, turning to Gareth.

'I'll ask Mrs Davies at school, her brother works at the Museum in Cardiff and took us round on our school visit,' said Gareth.

'And now for goodness sake, let's go to bed. I feel as though I've been awake for three days.' Dad rose tiredly to his feet. 'And let's keep the cave and the coins a bit of a secret in the family, shall we, till we know the full story. I don't want newspapermen and people with metal detectors all over my land upsetting the ewes and lambs. That means you too, Bethan, no phoning Rhian Lewis or it will be all over Wales by dawn.' Bethan gave Dad an angry glare and flounced off to her room. Her nose really had been put out of joint.

The first thing Gareth did next morning was to look and see if his pot of coins was still there. It was. He hadn't dreamt it after all.

Gareth tipped out the coins again and looked at them in daylight. There were faint letters round the edges but he couldn't make out any words, just a few

46

47

letters, T then a C then a D then a C. It was so frustrating, worse than finding wrapped hidden presents under Mam's bed and having to wait until Christmas Day.

He wanted to phone Mrs Davies, but Mam said Mrs Davies probably had problems of her own with the floods and surely Gareth could wait a day or two. But he was allowed to phone Tada who was so excited that he dropped his pipe into his cup of tea, and wanted to come over to the farm right away to see for himself. But of course he couldn't because of the floods.

All day his family, the neighbouring farmers and the TV and radio were preoccupied with the floods. No one gave a second thought to the old coins Gareth had found. But Gareth was thinking about his discovery all the time. He was trying to work out how they got into the cave. Who could have put them there?

He discussed his ideas with Caradoc who blinked his green eyes and pretended to listen. There were some interruptions to these discussions because Caradoc seemed to think there was a mouse behind the wardrobe and needed Gareth's help. After much heaving and pushing the mousehole was visible for Caradoc to watch over. The back of the wardrobe had some enormous spiders too and Gareth wondered if he could train them for racing. Perhaps not, there had been such a fuss when the racing snails escaped. In any case his find in the cave was much more important at the moment.

Would they have been bank robbers? But not modern ones, they wouldn't put money in a pot. Highwaymen Gareth considered, were a possibility. And what about medieval barons and knights or fleeing Roundheads and Cavaliers?

Gareth liked the idea of a highwayman and imagined himself as one galloping up the mountainside on a black horse looking for somewhere to stow his loot. By the light of the full moon he saw the cave and crept into it, feeling around the walls for a place to hide the pot. He found the little shelf and hid the pot. Then he galloped away to rob some more rich people. But he never returned because he was hanged at the gallows. Gareth imagined the noose around his neck. Then he remembered the little lamp, which wasn't a bit like a highwayman's equipment. So that idea was no good.

If it wasn't a highwayman, perhaps it had been stolen from an abbey or monastery by robbers. It didn't seem to be English money, so perhaps it was foreign and had been brought over by people running away from danger in their own countries?

Gareth tried to remember if Robin Hood had ever come to Wales and robbed rich nobles.

By bedtime Gareth's head was in such a whirl with theories about his find that he tossed and turned all night. A great procession of robbers, knights, monks, barons and highwaymen rode through his bedroom, each rattling a money pot. He woke up once and wished he'd not had such a very large piece of cheese before going to bed. Mam had warned him he would dream.

Chapter Five

The next day the local radio announced that the roads were open and all schools and school buses were back to normal. Gareth put a gold and a silver coin in a pouch on a bit of string round his neck. Mam had given him the pouch to keep inside his shirt to make sure he didn't lose his coins.

Well, he would know that morning whether his coins were important or not. The suspense was almost unbearable.

He was first in the bus queue. After the flood everything looked soggy. There was mud on the road and branches of trees lying in the fields. Along the river bank plastic fertiliser and animal feed bags which had been washed downstream from farmyards were hanging on the bushes like orange and blue flags waiting for a race. And the river itself was racing. It had gone back into its course but it was full to the brim and a horrible brown colour. All kinds of objects were floating down; more tree trunks, bits of garden shed and hen pens and even a pram. Gareth hoped the baby had been rescued.

In school the rain had come in through a broken window and Mrs Davies was terribly busy sorting out wet books and papers, so the class had to write an account of their experiences in the floods. Gareth could write pages and pages normally, but that day he could only manage half a page, starting 'We had to rescue the sheep.' It sounded dreadfully dull but his mind was full of his great news which he had promised Dad he wouldn't tell to half the school. Not even to Gethin. He'd never had to keep a secret for this long and he felt about to explode. Perhaps this was how Bethan felt when she said she was stressed!

He dawdled so much at break that his friends went off without him but at last he caught Mrs Davies alone.

'Look,' was all he said as he held out the two coins in the palm of his hand.

Mrs Davies patted a wisp of hair into place and looked, and looked again. She picked up the gold coin and turned it over carefully.

'Gareth, where on earth did these come from?'

So he explained and Mrs Davies listened.

'I think these are Roman coins, Gareth, and probably almost two thousand years old. You may have found something very, very important. Would it be alright if I phone your parents tonight? This sort of thing has to be investigated by experts, you know. And don't tell anyone about it yet.' Mrs Davies's wisps of hair stuck out in a halo right round her head, she was so excited.

When Mrs Davies said 'Roman,' something stirred in Gareth's memory. Of course, all those centurions in armour with plumed helmets walking along straight roads and building forts and conquering the Ancient Britons. And there was Julius Caesar and Rome and emperors, it was all coming back to him. He'd clean forgotten that Romans used coins. Probably the forts and the soldiers had been much more interesting so that he hadn't bothered with the coins.

But Romans in this valley, no one had ever mentioned them before!

The bell sounded and boys and girls started to drift back into the classroom. Gareth put his coins away quickly. He had missed break but it didn't matter at all today; but he wondered how much longer he could keep his secret.

Gethin was curious. 'What were you and Mrs Davies pow-wowing about at break? Something's up, isn't it?'

'Well, yes and no,' said Gareth. 'I can't tell you yet, I've promised Mam and Dad.'

'I thought we were best mates and shared things,' said Gethin sulkily.

'Yes, we are, but I've promised Mam and Dad. You'll be the first to know after them. Promise.'

And Gethin had to be content with that. Gareth

began to worry about his secret. It was bursting to come out like a chicken out of an egg. Gareth thought it must be very difficult being a spy. And a Prime Minister must find it terribly difficult in case he let out any State Secrets. Gareth felt it was even harder for him because he'd never had to keep a big secret before.

That evening, Mrs Davies was as good as her word and phoned Mam. It was arranged that Mrs Davies's brother from Cardiff would come the next day. And Gareth was allowed a day off from school for such an important visit. Better still, a real archaeologist was coming with him who was a professor. Gareth wondered what the professor would look like—the ones on TV were a bit peculiar looking sometimes with lots of wild hair and beards.

Next morning Mam fussed about giving the parlour table a polish and putting daffodils on the windowsill. Then she made Welsh cakes and sponges and cut piles of sandwiches. 'They'll be hungry with all the mountain air, and it's a long way from Cardiff,' she said, but Gareth knew she loved visitors to their lonely farm. Mam had worked in a busy bank in Builth before she married Dad and still missed seeing lots of people every day.

By two o'clock all was ready. The pot of coins sat in the middle of the kitchen table. It all looked very important.

The visitors arrived in a muddy old Landrover. Mrs Davies' brother got out first; he was stout and jolly. A tall man unfolded his legs from the car and was introduced as Dr Griffiths, Professor of Archaeology from the University. He was quite young, no frizzy hair or anything peculiar, but he was very tall. He wore a battered tweed jacket, which had a button missing just at Gareth's eye level.

Gareth began to feel nervous. Suppose his find was just some stupid joke someone had buried only ten years ago! He was glad Caradoc was there. He stroked him hard which was very comforting.

Mam and Dad sat the visitors round the kitchen table and made polite grown-up conversation about the weather and the floods. But Gareth noticed the Professor's eyes were on the little pot.

Then the Professor smiled encouragingly at him, 'Now, Gareth, show us this exciting find of yours.'

Gareth gave a quick hitch to his spectacles and slowly emptied the pot out onto the table. Then the Professor took off his spectacles and polished them and put them back on. Gareth held his breath. Any second now he would know. The Professor cleared his throat.

'Well, the pot is a Roman money pot, now let's try the coins.' He picked up a gold one first. 'Yes, this is an *aureus*, a gold coin. This is an emperor's head on the back, the Roman emperor Claudius who invaded Britain in the year 43. You can only just see the letters TICLAUDCAESAR round the edge of the coin. Claudius was his first name and Caesar was the Roman emperor's surname. At least that's how we would call them today.'

The Professor stopped and looked over his spectacles at Gareth 'I expect you have heard of Julius Caesar, haven't you?'

Gareth nodded.

The Professor turned the gold coin over, 'And here's the goddess of victory. See her wings and a laurel crown, and she's holding a palm tree in her hand.'

His spectacles were steaming up with excitement and the warm kitchen, and he stopped to polish them. Gareth polished his as well, which made him feel a bit like an archaeologist too.

Gareth craned forward eagerly, keen to see the marks on the tiny coin which the Professor was explaining so easily. Gareth thought he must be awfully clever to know so much. Even Mrs Davies's brother was looking impressed. Mam and Dad were looking completely bewildered by all the Latin names.

But now the Professor was rummaging in the dull

metal coins with his long fingers. 'Mm,' he said, 'these are silver denarii, even the black tarnished ones. They have the Emperor Augustus's head on the back and his name on the front. Can you see the mythical animal with a fish tail and horns? It's holding the world in its hand and a horn of plenty over its shoulder.'

Again Gareth peered over the Professor's shoulder. He was fascinated by these strange names and gods.

'But how did they get into the cave?' asked Gareth.

'Hadn't we better go and inspect the cave?' suggested the Professor, looking at Dad.

Mam excused herself and bustled off to get the tea ready while the three of them put on boots and Dad collected a pickaxe and spade in case they had to move any rock.

Gareth started off up the path towards the cave. Would the hillside have slipped again and covered everything with earth? Would there be anything more to find on the second visit?

Chapter Six

The landslide on top of the cave was just as they had left it. After the rain stopped the earth and rock seemed to have settled and it looked safe. Nevertheless, Dad and the two visitors dug and pulled very carefully in case there was another fall. At last the cave opening was big enough for a man to enter.

The Professor looked round. 'It's your cave, Gareth, show us the way,' and he handed Gareth his torch.

Gareth felt very proud; he was actually going to show a *real* archaeologist his find. He climbed over the rock debris and pointed to the passage where he had found the coins. They trod carefully over the stony floor and into the passage; the men had to stoop as they were much taller than Gareth. He found the hiding place and shone the torch into it.

The Professor put his hand in and brought out the little Aladdin lamp. 'Ah,' he breathed 'a Roman oil lamp.' He took the torch from Gareth and peered again inside but there was nothing else. Then he crept up and down the passage examining the walls and picking up bits of the rock on the floor. He didn't say much, but kept nodding to Mrs Davies's brother and saying, 'This looks promising.'

It was stuffy in the cave and they were glad to get out into the fresh air after half an hour or so. Gareth could scarcely curb his impatience, he so wanted to know about his cave. The Professor saw that he was dying to know and after dusting bits of earth and rock off himself, he sat down on a flat rock to tell Gareth about it.

'This isn't a cave at all, Gareth; it's a Roman iron mine. We know there was a great Roman fort at Caerleon not so many miles from here and there were smaller forts at Abergavenny and Brecon. And the Romans had iron mines in the Forest of Dean. Some Roman soldiers and officials didn't go back to Rome when they retired, they stayed in Britain. I expect a few thought they would try iron mining. There might even have been a Roman smelting furnace in this valley and a settlement.'

'Then,' said Gareth, 'there are some more things to find?'

'Very probably. Archaeologists haven't really explored this valley but we have suspected that there might have been mining in the area because there is iron ore around here.' The Professor explained things patiently, and in a way that did not make anyone else feel foolish for knowing so little.

'But the coins and the pot, what have they got to do with the mine?' Gareth was very puzzled. 'Did

60

the miners make the coins, did they find gold and silver too?.

'One question at a time,' the Professor laughed. 'No, the coins would have been minted in Rome and brought to Britain to pay the soldiers and officials. I expect the miner had saved his pay and wanted a safe place to keep it and he used the mine. There wouldn't have been any banks up here then, you know.'

'Why didn't he collect it?' asked Gareth.

'Who knows, perhaps he died suddenly and no one else knew it was there;' said the Professor.

'Can we find out?' asked Gareth.

'We'll have to see.' said the Professor.

They walked back to the farm, the Professor and Mrs Davies's brother looking at the mountains and the valley all the time, and asking Dad questions about them.

Mam met them at the door. 'Now I'm sure you all need some tea after that. The kettle's just boiled and everything's ready. Take them into the parlour, Gareth will you'

Gareth did as he was told, but his heart sank. He wanted to ask the Professor so many questions and there was Mam organising everyone as usual. He wanted to know about everything. His head felt like a giant question mark. Why were the gods and goddesses used on coins? Why was the money made

61

in Rome and not in Wales? Could the coins be used now? And who was the Roman miner?

Gareth sighed. The Professor heard his sigh and winked at him. Gareth thought, he knows what it's like—perhaps he had a Mam who fussed and grumbled about muddy clothes and things.

Dad came back in for tea too, after he had seen to the sheep. As the sandwiches and cakes disappeared and third cups of tea were poured, Dad asked the one question which really interested him.

'Well now, is this a Treasure Trove we've got or just a few bits?' he asked stirring his tea.

'Oh, it's definitely a Treasure Trove,' said the Professor, 'most buried gold and silver is. And it will have to be dealt with officially. First of all it has to be reported to the Police and then to the Coroner. Then there will be an Inquest with an archaeologist present, to decide whether the coins were thrown away, or lost, or buried to be recovered one day. I expect they were hidden in the cave to be recovered, so they still belong to the Roman miner.'

'Well we can't trace him, can we?' said Dad. 'So I suppose it will belong to us as it's on our land.'

'Afraid not,' said the Professor. 'If the miner's successors can't be traced, which we know is impossible, the Treasure goes to the Crown. But the Crown does give a Reward for things, you know, and a Museum would buy the coins in due course I expect.'

Mrs Davies's brother nodded in agreement. 'Of course it would take time, but you would be paid eventually.'

'But,' went on the Professor, 'I have a small team of young archaeologists ready to dig in the summer and this would make an excellent area for them to work in. My problem is that they are only students and there aren't many grants available, and hotels are so expensive. I suppose you don't know of a farm which does bed and breakfast and supper at a reasonable rate, do you?' He looked hopefully at Mam.

Mam caught Dad's eye. 'Well there's this farmhouse. We can sleep an extra six if they'll share a room—good plain country food, nothing fancy, mind,' Mam said.

'If your plain country food is anything like your tea, we'll be fed like Roman emperors,' said the Professor. 'I'm sure it would be just right for us.'

Gareth had noticed the Professor had an enormous appetite; he'd eaten four slices of *bara brith*, two Welsh cakes, and two pieces of chocolate sponge, as well as sandwiches. Gareth wondered if all archaeologists were thin and hungry.

Gareth could sense that Mam's mind had become

a cross between a cash register and a cookery book; she would love the cooking and the company. And the extra money would buy the new washing machine she kept saying she needed.

The Professor looked at Gareth. 'Have you anything lined up for the summer, Gareth? Camping or the seaside or anything?'

Gareth shook his head, 'I've no one to go with, and Mam and Dad can't leave the farm.'

'I'm sure the archaeological team could use a boy for the summer,' said the professor, looking thoughtfully at Gareth.

'You mean I can come help and look for things and dig properly?' Gareth cried, his spectacles sliding right off the end of his nose in his excitement. The Professor nodded smiling.

When the Professor and Mrs Davies's brother had gone, promising to be in touch again soon, Gareth went up to his room. With Caradoc a warm bundle in his arms he sat and looked at at the pot, the little oil lamp and the heap of coins which were opening up a whole new world for him.

The Professor had promised to send him some more books about Romans. When Gareth, full of embarrassment, said he hadn't any savings to pay for new books at the moment because of the bother with Caradoc and the fish, the Professor said of course the books would be a present, and one of them he'd actually written himself.

The Professor hadn't been a bit weird and Mam and Dad had taken to him too. He'd even had a chat in Welsh with Mam. Gareth had overhead a particularly interesting conversation about food. Mam's best Welsh recipes were mentioned; *cawl, cig oen rhost, crempog, teisen lap, pwdin reis Mamgu, pice ar y maen, tarten gennin, tatws popty*. She even mentioned curries and beans on toast. The Professor had been nodding away with a big smile on his face. Gareth's stomach gave a somersault at the thought of all the lovely food to come.

He wondered what the student archaeologists would be like. He hoped there wouldn't be any grumpy sister types with them. They would get very dirty digging and on their hands and knees scraping away with trowels. Mam wouldn't be able to scold *them* and if he was digging too she wouldn't be able to scold him either.

As for Bethan and David, they wouldn't dare scoff at him in future. And Tada, Tada would be thrilled to bits and want to come back to stay and dig too, and blow to his rheumatics.

When the news of the discovery would eventually come out, Gareth would have his name in the local *Chronicle*. Maybe he would be on TV in 'Wales

Tonight'! But that mightn't be so good: Mam would want him all washed and clean if he was to be seen on TV.

The Professor had suggested there could be more Roman remains around the farm, a road or a farm or even a small fort. Gareth could imagine a villa, a Roman Bath too. Perhaps when the archaeological team had finished, the Professor would write a book, with Gareth's help of course, and his name would appear on the front page—'Assisted by Gareth Morgan'. He would be famous.

Gareth closed his eyes in bliss. What a summer he was going to have. Loads of food, getting dirty, and best of all, he would learn how to be an archaeologist right here in his own valley.

Here is a list of the books the Professor sent to Gareth. If you would you like to read them, ask for help at your local library.

What do we know about the Romans? MARTEN, H. (Simon & Schuster)

History as Evidence: The Romans (Kingfisher) CORBISHLEY, M.

Face to Face: Romans & Celts MACDONALD, F. (Simon & Schuster)

The Legionary CONNOLLY, P. (Oxford Univ.Pr.)

The Cavalryman CONNOLLY, P. (Oxford Univ.Pr.).

Rome and Romans (Usborne)

The Romans in Wales (Univ. Wales Pr.)

See Inside series: *A Roman town* (Kingfisher)

Rome and the Ancient World Illustrated History of the World: (Simon & Schuster)

Roman Coins relating to Britain BESLEY, E. (National Museum of Wales)

Some Welsh words are used in this story. Their meanings are as follows:

bach ⎫	both are used like the English
cariad ⎭	word 'love' when speaking
	to someone e.g. 'Are you hungry, love?'
Duw	God
tadcu (Tada)	grandfather
bara brith	fruit loaf, spread with butter
cawl	broth/soup
cig oen rhost	roast lamb
crempog	pancakes
pice ar y maen	Welsh cakes
pwdin reis Mamgu	Grandmother's rice pudding
tarten gennin	leek tart
tatws popty	baked potatoes
teisen lap	currant cake

OTHER TITLES

ISBN 1 85902 727 X

£3.95

The best thing (and the worst thing) about Josh is that he
believes he can do everything in the world. Even difficult
things. Even flying machines.
'He's crazy,' says Tim.

Of course, that means Tim's crazy too,
for joining in. But people just can't help
getting involved once Josh starts on a project. Even Siân admits
that, although she has other things on her mind this summer
holiday.

At Tenby, a film is being shot and Siân is taken on as an extra.
It's her big chance to mix with the stars, one of whom is
behaving very strangely indeed. When Siân next sees Tim
and Josh, she has an important and very surprising message for
them . . .

ISBN 0 86383 990 8

£3.95

When Denny's parents have problems, he goes to live
with his grandmother in Owen Street. She's kind, a brilliant cook and
sometimes seems to Denny even younger than
his mother.
But even she is exasperated when Denny turns up plastered in mud after
'going over the tide', walking the muddy shoreline of the Taff mouth.
Before the wild tide-fields
are turned into concrete and tarmac Denny is determined to enjoy the
natural untideness of it and can't keep away.
'Now listen to me, my boy. The river fascinates you.
I know that. But it's dangerous! It can change in a second – and sweep
you away. Denny – children have been drowned in the Taff! You've been
warned all your life.
You know about that treacherous old tide.
So why do you go there?'

The author, Pamela Purnell, was born in Cardiff where
she spent her childhood. She too lived near the
River Taff estuary.

ISBN 1 85902 000 3

£4.50

Daniel is ten years old but is 'inclined to be small and skinny' and feels a real towny when he goes to stay on his Uncle's sheep farm. Despite the protection of his cousin Robin and the kindness of his Auntie Mair, he does not like farm work, fears his gruff uncle, 'Jac Hendre' and is rather lonely.

Then the Old Man of Gilfach — 'a crazy old crackpot' to some people — enters his life and teaches him about the old Welsh ways and the care of wild creatures. Most important, he introduces him to the ravens. It is the Old Man and a raven called 'Krawk' who captivate Daniel and help him to know himself and to gain confidence and courage.